SPANKING THE GOOD GIRL

AN OFFICE PUNISHMENT EROTIC NOVELLETE

CLARA COLT

1
———

I woke up late with a hangover and realised I would either have to pay for a cab to get to work on time or skip short on my make-up and hair.

Of course this was to be my very first day as a junior P.A. at Quant, a very upmarket finance research firm where everyone looked like money.

Not, I thought glumly as I stared at my smeared eyeliner and wild bed-head in the bathroom, like a total disaster.

But that was me, princess of disasters. Ever since I dropped out of university three credits short of graduating because I was *so* sure I was crazy in love with the wrong guy, I seemed to have bounced from one bad decision to another. And last night's decision to celebrate my fancy new job with a party had definitely been a bad idea.

Still, at least this time I'd ended up back in my own bed and alone. I was decided. No more one night stands with strangers. I was going to be a Good Girl from now on. Professional and focused.

I chanted that inside my head as I dragged my straightener through my natural blonde waves, grateful at least that I didn't have to worry about roots. And I was still young enough that I could get away with a lick of blush and some deep red lipstick only.

I pulled out the work-appropriate suit I'd scored on a bargain price after some serious hunting. Little navy pencil skirt, silky white blouse and a pair of four-inch heels that while I couldn't run in, did set my hips off to a sexy sway. I'd seen what the other women on staff were wearing when I went in for my final interview the previous week, and I needed to look sharp, not dowdy.

I still hadn't met my actual boss though, just his senior P.A.. She'd been a stunning redhead and I'd felt like a washed out check-out girl next to her effortless class, because as of yesterday, that's exactly what I had been. Bagging groceries and handing out receipts where the highlight of my day was getting first dibs on the free samples.

But finally, a break. I still wasn't sure why she'd picked me out of all the other sleek professional women waiting for interviews in the lobby. We'd been milling about, staring daggers at each other, or rather they had at me with my chipped manicure and cheap shoes.

Well, I'd fixed the manicure as best I could with the help of my roommate Trissy, so it was time for me to quit biting my nails, eat my vegetables and do whatever it was Good Girls do.

Be punctual? I thought catching sight of my alarm clock. I was definitely going to be late if I didn't get a move on.

In the kitchen, Trissy was drinking coffee and wordlessly held out a travel mug to me as I rushed in. "You look very not you, Sabina" she said. "Totally stuck up. Have a great first day!"

I ran down the staircase from our dingy apartment and hailed a cab. As I got in, my legs slid across the over-heated vinyl on the back seat and I realised that I'd forgotten to wear pantyhose.

My legs are probably my favourite feature because I used to run track and still go for regular runs so they've got defined muscles. I'm taller than most girls which intimidates most men unfortunately, but all that means is that I've got miles of long lovely legs.

That looked great in the little pencil skirt, but pretty unprofessional. I waxed so they were lovely and smooth, but still absolutely bare. I wondered if they would be polite enough to ignore this or if I'd get a note from HR on professional work standards?

It was too late to head back as the cab was pulling into the front of the gleaming glass tower where Quant took up the two top floors.

I was working for one of the directors, a Tomas R. Perrington. Even his name sounded fancy, and I was hoping he'd turn out to be a little nicer and easier than it suggested. I could do with a better boss. My last job as a P.A. had been to a cold-hearted witch and her awful husband who had made me do all their errands, babysit their horrible children and keep their office running smoothly. Quitting that job and going to work at a supermarket had been a relief.

But this job paid well with benefits, and it was kinda nice to be in such a posh place, I mused as I strode through the lobby, surreptitiously tugging down my skirt to cover more of my bare legs.

They had my new security card at the desk, complete with a photograph I'd sent in where I looked more like a startled deer than a real human. Still, it got me past the turnstiles and into the mirrored elevators, crowded with business suits and briefcases.

I had a tote bag from the library. I know, super classy. But until my first pay cheque came in, there was no way I could afford a decent bag.

Bing We had arrived. Now on my second visit to the Quant offices, I could take a moment to look around. It was busy, but that expensive calm busy where everyone seems to know where they're going with a purpose. The receptionist was a stunning woman with dark skin and amber eyes, her make-up so flawless I thought she had to have been a model at some point.

I showed her my badge and explained I was the new P.A. for Mr Perrington and one eyebrow tilted ever so little. "Ah, Sabina the new junior P.A." she said. "His office is the final door down that corridor. Knock and wait for him to call you."

She pointed at a long carpeted corridor lined with doors and artwork. The corridor seemed to go on forever, or that was just my nerves. By the time I did reach the final door, bigger and darker than the rest, I was starting to feel a knot in my stomach.

No-one I'd passed had said anything. Their gazes had just slid over me as though I wasn't even visible. And yet, I felt like I was being watched.

Standing outside the door, I knocked twice. Then I glanced up and froze. There was a discrete small camera near the ceiling. Looking back over my shoulder I could see more of them, tucked away but clearly observing the entire office. Paranoid much? Maybe they had serious security concerns.

"Enter," growled a deep voice. I took a deep breath and opened the door.

The man inside wasn't anything like the fussy elderly gentleman I'd pictured. For starters, he was huge, at least six foot-six with broad shoulders that a well tailored suit did little to hide. There were muscles under that fine tailoring, I was sure. He looked as though someone had taken a wild bear and somehow barely tamed it, all raw shaggy power compressed into one fierce glaring face.

He wasn't exactly handsome. His nose was a little crooked from where it must've been broken a few times, and his eyes were too brooding to be handsome. But he had a raw intense presence that made him magnetic.

The top button of his crisp striped shirt was open, his silk tie loosened, and I could just see the barest hint of chest hair. I wanted suddenly to be able to pull open that tie, tear open that shirt and see just what the rest of his chest was like. Muscled, hairy and scarred. For some reason, I found myself thinking of brutal hand to hand fighting.

Not finance, for sure. I was standing by the door, gaping and he said irritably, "Close the door."

I did and then we were alone, my new boss and I.

"You're late," he said. His voice was a real growl, resonating through me. I couldn't explain the heat I felt when he rolled his r's, the way he seemed to savour each word with utter finality. Just that I wanted to hear him speaking. Whispering into my ear.

"I'm sorry, sir," I said. "I took a taxi but the traffic —"

He waved his hand dismissively. "I don't care about excuses," he said. "You're late and this is your one warning."

"Yes, sir," I said. "Mr Perrington."

His eyes darkened. "Sir is acceptable."

My mouth was dry. "Sir," I managed.

"You'll be working at a desk over there," he said and pointed. There was a tiny little desk tucked away in the far corner of his office. I was surprised — usually P.A.s get a desk outside the office for the boss' privacy, especially anyone as minor as a junior P.A. but I guess he wanted me close to hand.

His gaze raked me up and down. "You're also not dressed appropriately."

I blushed, and looked down at my bare legs. Did he mean them or was he criticising my clothes? I knew compared to the other women in the office I was woefully underdressed, but I honestly couldn't afford more.

He pulled open a desk drawer at his enormous metal desk and tossed a packet from it across to me. It skidded on the floor and rested near my shoe.

The box was almost austere in its plainness, only the words "lingerie" written in a simple script across the front. I glanced at my boss who did nothing but stare implacably back at me in silence, then picked it up.

Inside the box were a pair of tights. They were different to the cheap supermarket pantyhose I had at home. These were definitely silk from the cool glide they made across my hand when I held them. A long dark seam ran up them to the top which was embroidered all over. They had tiny clips and when I looked into the box, I found a matching garter belt.

"Um, I can go and get dressed now?" I asked, unsure what to do with the handful of silk lingerie he had casually thrown at me.

"You were late," he said and he leaned forward on the desk, lacing his hands together. He looked as calm as if he was discussing the weather, not telling me to get changed in front of him. "Get changed here."

My breath hitched. Was this some kind of weird punishment? I'd been late by maybe two minutes. There was no way he really meant for me to put on the stockings in front of him. Surely.

But he just waited, staring at me without moving. I felt caught in his gaze, prey before predator. And even stranger, part of me wanted to.

So much for the Good Girl mantra.

Part of me, the part that had throbbed when he first growled at me to call him Sir, wanted to show him that I wasn't some timid little prude who would run off to HR.

I stepped out of my shoes, bare feet luxuriating in the feel of the very thick Persian rug he had laid out on his office floor. His eyes tracked my legs and I stood a little straighter.

Pulling them on without wobbling side to side took concentration. I wasn't used to a garter belt either. I worked up my skirt first, rolling it above my hips so that the little bright pink panties I was wearing that morning were visible. Then, one hand sliding up and down my long smooth thigh, I fastened the belt around my waist and arranged it so all the little straps hung just so.

He was definitely leaning forward. He hadn't spoken and neither did I.

I bent over a little, making sure that my shirt swooped down to show off my cleavage while I rolled the first stocking over my toes and pulled it up past my calves to the gentle swell of my thigh. I gasped a little; I couldn't help it, the silk felt so luxurious against my skin.

Then I balanced on the other foot and repeated, but this time, I did it a little slower, stretched my leg out first to admire the way the stockings looked over my legs, before

I straightened my skirt back down and stepped back into my shoes.

I knew that my panties were wet now. Something forbidden had already happened inside the office and just the heat from him watching me had me worked up. I could smell my own desire and I wondered as he sat there, silently watching me, if he could too.

"What next, sir?" I asked, trying to sound calm and professional even though I wanted to moan from the sweet silky slide of my thighs against each other.

"Hmm," he said, leaning back in his big office chair. "You can start looking through my schedule. It's on the laptop at your desk."

I went over to the desk, making sure to sway my hips a little as I walked away from him. Part of me wondered if that was it, some hazing ritual that he did on every P.A.

Then I remembered what his senior P.A. had said when she hired me. "Mr Perrington is very particular about how his office works," she had said. "If you please him, he will treat you very well."

Apparently I'd been picked for more than my typing and organising skills. I remembered the way her cool eyes had flicked over me, assessing my body and looks. I'd felt embarrassed, too tall and with big breasts, more stripper than secretary material. But it turned out I was exactly what he'd wanted.

Or I would be. I thought of my bills waiting to be paid and heading back out into the job market. Maybe

Perrington was a little kinky, but I could handle him, I was sure.

That was Monday.

2

————————

On Tuesday, I forgot to bring his coffee with two shots of espresso and had to stand absolutely still in the middle of the room while he circled me. He didn't do anything, didn't touch me, but merely came closer and closer until all my skin was prickling with maddened desire, wanting him to touch me. I was sure from the way he leaned in and breathed at the nap of my neck, a hot heat on my skin that made my nipples tighten, that he could smell my desire.

But he didn't touch me.

On Wednesday, I did everything he asked perfectly and he ignored me. That was worse.

On Thursday, I came in early and by the afternoon, just being around him and feeling the silky shimmer of the stockings rubbing together every time I moved in my chair I was desperate.

It was a quiet afternoon. He'd had meetings all morning and the next hour was blocked out for him to work. He preferred taking notes with an old-fashioned fountain pen, notes that I would type up later for him. It suited him, those massive hands holding a fine pen with such finesse that all I could think of was how he would handle me.

I went to fetch his afternoon coffee and a mad idea came to me as I was carrying it back to the office.

I needed the job, I really did. But my brain was no longer in control, not around him. My body was.

I stood in front of his desk, holding the cup of coffee. "Sir, your coffee," I said and then deliberately, slowly, poured it down my front.

I was wearing a narrow white dress that day, something prim and proper. It soaked completely through, the hot coffee warm and wet on my front, dripping down my legs onto the carpet.

Mr Perrington didn't move for a moment. Then he sighed and put down his pen and stood up. He took off his jacket and folded it across the back of his chair.

He came around the desk and leaned back against it, watching me standing there wet and rapidly growing cold in the chilly office. My dress was ruined of course, and it was practically transparent at the front, revealing that all I was wearing below was the garter belt and the silk stockings.

Then, without warning, he slapped me. It wasn't a light slap either. My ears rang and I tasted a tiny bit of blood from my inner cheek. It wasn't brutal either, just enough that I felt burned hot and stinging.

Then his hand was cradling the other side of my face, catching the hot tears escaping from me, and he was blowing gently on the red of my cheek. It felt like I was half on fire, half caressed and confused the hell out of me before melting into a sweet sharp pain.

"Little mess," he said almost fondly. He pressed his mouth to the edge of my jaw, his teeth tracing against the tender skin there, licking and nipping. I let out a sigh and reached for him but he caught my wrists and held me at a distance.

"Patience," he said and I stilled.

We stared at each other, the heat between us rising. He held my wrists lightly. If I tugged my hands loose, I knew he would let me go. He would let me gather myself in dignity and walk to the door and leave.

I would not have to come back. I thought of all those other women that his senior P.A. had examined and found wanting. What was it she had seen in me that made her choose me for her boss?

What was it that made me lick my dry lips and nod, obediently?

He lowered my hands and crossed them over my front. "Stay," he ordered and I felt a new thrill come on, one I hadn't experienced before.

There had been men who liked to boss me around in bed of course, but never someone who had been able to hold me absolutely still with just their voice. Not until Sir and his deep rumble of a growl.

And the promise of a tight slap if I disobeyed.

Part of me wanted to move, but my face was still deliciously hot and I could feel my body trembling, wanting to know what would happen if I obeyed. If I was his Good Girl.

"Better," he whispered and then he was behind me and unzipping my dress. It came down and I was left in my bra and stockings.

The bra, he slid his hand up my back and under the strap to unhook. His hands were so big that he could span my entire back. I felt like he was branding me from the heat of his outstretched hand against my back.

More than that, I wanted to lean back against them, to have me hold me, catch me up in his arms. He was so massively built and *male*, and I wanted him to enfold me completely within those muscled arms so that I was protected.

Protected. How could I feel this way about a man who slapped me? But he was right, I'd brought it on myself, daring him by deliberately pouring coffee down my front.

And I was still wet and sticky from the coffee.

He unpeeled my bra from my body. The feel of the damp lace across my achingly hard nipples was a new subtle torture. He threw my bra aside and then it was just me in the stockings he'd given me.

He was so close behind me I could feel the heat coming off his body. Part of me didn't want any of him to get mussed up, to leave him as immaculate and perfect as he was. And part of me wanted him as dirty and messy as me, ruining all of his handsome suit by fucking me hard over his desk.

I waited, quivering with desire, as he made up his mind what to do with me.

"You're filthy," he said. "A filthy, dirty little slut."

His hand went up to the nape of my hair and grabbed the chignon I had carefully swept my hair into. Roughly he pulled it out and then took hold of my hair, arching me back. I was almost falling, the high heels I wore and the way he was bending me back. I knew what I must look like, curved over, breasts jutting and jiggling as he bent my face round.

Then he kissed me and I didn't care how much it hurt. All I knew was the taste of his tongue plundering my mouth, the rasp of his beard against me. He kissed like I wanted him to fuck me, hard and dirty and rough. Every now and then, when I was almost relaxing into that heady warmth, he would twist his hand in my hair, sending little shivers of pain-pleasure through me. I moaned into his mouth, begging for more.

"Good girl," he said when he finally left my mouth bruised with he force of his kisses. "Now bend over and hold onto the desk."

I knew that he had a meeting in less than twenty minutes. How was I supposed to get cleaned up in time, how was he going to — and then his hand ran down my back and cupped the cheek of my arse and squeezed like I was a ripe peach he was testing. His thumb ran along the edge of my garter belt and lifted it slightly, let it fall with a tight snap.

Suddenly I didn't give a damn who walked in. I just knew I had to obey him.

I bent over and gripped the edge of his desk. The metal was cold under my fingers, just far enough away that I could only rest my fever-hot face against my outstretched arms, not on the cool surface of the desk itself.

My hands trembled. My knees were weak. I was so aroused by then that he could have done nothing at all but gently breathed on my cunt and I would've come. It was torturous to just wait, to hear the little soft sounds he made moving behind me.

And then, oh then most wonderful of all… the slow deliberate rasp of his zipper going down. I groaned and arched my back even more, widening my legs open for him.

The back of his hand came down on my arse again, then both hands and he was squeezing and spreading me open. His big strong fingers massaged the firm flesh of my arse, then his thumbs moved down and brushed the wet folds of my cunt. It was pure pleasure, having him rub just the edges of the soaked lips, teasing me as he circled my waiting cunt.

I wanted to see but I knew if I raised my head or turned around, that I'd be punished again, and I wanted him even more.

"You're wet," he said approvingly and I thrilled at that tone. I wanted to do whatever he asked. "Are you wet enough though."

Then I felt him right at my cunt, this enormous blunt cocked pushing, pushing into me. I was wet but I didn't know if I could take him, he was so huge. I gasped and bit into my arm to stop from screaming. It burned almost, but then he spread one hand under me, his clever thumb stroking my clit in the same heavy intense rhythm that he was beginning to fuck into me with.

I groaned and pushed back, willing myself to relax into him. Slowly, every thrust burying him a little deeper, he worked his way into my tight hot cunt. I was so close to coming by then, not even fully fucked by him, because he moved with such iron control.

All of me, from my breasts swinging in time to the steady thrusts, my arse driving back against him, his hand cradling the mound of my pubis, finger delving into the curls there to find my clit and winding me into sweet, sweet release.

All of me was narrowed down to that cock splitting me open. That huge slow pounding as he fucked into me. I was liquid, molten over him and barely able to stay upright, it felt so good. So intense.

"Hold tighter," he commanded and I gripped the desk with white knuckles. He was buried completely inside me now. I could feel him jutting up into my belly, buried to the hilt. His balls nestled right at my cunt and I wished wildly that I could somehow be on my knees before him, have him fucking my mouth so I could touch them and lick them and love them.

I wanted him everywhere.

But then he withdrew, just the very tip of him rubbing against my aching hole, sore from that huge gorgeous cock. I cried out and he put his hand warningly on the back of my neck, pushing my head down. "Quiet, little mess," he said.

I found I liked that. Liked being his little mess. Liked the feel of his hand steady and enormous on my head so that all I could do was helplessly push back up. I was trapped between his body and his desk, and I wanted to be.

I was quiet and he stroked the back of my head for a moment, his hand gentle as he cradled where he'd slapped me. I pressed a kiss against his palm, grateful.

Then he gripped my hips and sank himself in to the hilt. It was fast, it was rough and it was hard. I screamed because it was so good. It was the kind of deep heavy thrust that filled me up and made my thighs shake. I didn't know I could take such a huge cock, or how much I would enjoy it.

Then he was fucking into me again and again, a savage pounding. I held on to the desk and tried not to scream again, tried to stay quiet like he'd ordered me, but it was the hardest thing in the world when it felt so good. He would pull all the way out, leaving me shattered and empty, then sink his fingers down into my hips and slam his cock back in to ride me hard again.

My orgasm came fast, driven into me with his cock and the slow sweet burn of the bruises on my hips. It wasn't the quick simple orgasms I usually had. No, this came in a rush from my cunt, a wave of heat that built up and exploded, dark sugar sweet through my veins and left me gasping and writhing within his arms.

I was still impaled by his cock, still trapped within the steel cage of his arms around my hips. I sobbed, trying to let go of the desk and work myself onto his cock, to find release again. I was desperate for more.

He gave me more. He drew his cock out and then slowly, very slowly, drove back into me. "Stay still, little mess," he ordered again.

I tried to hold on to the desk, but my hand slipped. He leaned down, holding me tight around his cock with one hand while with his other, he gathered both of my wrists easily with his hands and pinned them to his chest. Now I was trapped against him. I could feel the cold metal of his open zipper now, the soft wool of his pants. He was fully clothed and here I was, naked and begging against him.

I clenched my inner muscles around him and he groaned and shifted. "You're not very obedient, are you, my little mess?" he whispered into my ear. I flexed again and again, squeezing his cock as hard as I could. There was just enough wriggle room in his grasp that I could almost work myself against him, a tiny movement up and down. I was aching for him to thrust again, for more.

But he stayed absolutely still. His cock was rock-hard and buried deep inside of me, and he knew it was torture. Knew how badly I wanted him from the way I writhed within his grasp.

"Please, Sir," I said. "Oh please."

He put my hands back on the desk and ran his fingers down my arched back towards my arse. Then I felt him spank me, a short sharp slaps on each bared arse cheek. The jolt of it was electric, wonderful. I moaned and wriggled back against his cock.

He drew his cock out and I begged. "Please, Sir. Please, again."

He spanked me again. Exactly on the same spot. Then he rubbed his hands over the reddened skin, a delicious over-sensitive touch. I moaned and he lifted up my hips, his fingers finding my clit again and teasing it almost painfully. I could feel his massive cock just rubbing up against my cunt, sliding against my wet thighs.

"You haven't behaved, little mess," he said as I rubbed shamelessly against his cock, as I gasped and moaned again and again for him to fuck me.

He sounded almost amused. Certain. I wanted to look back at him, but I was too lost in the pleasure of him finally fucking into me again and again. I began to come, and he pulled slowly out while I mewled for a deeper fucking, desperate for more. Then his fingers were on my cunt, and he had me screaming at the intensity of the orgasm he worked out of me.

I wanted more. But he knew it and he wouldn't give it to me. Knew I hadn't been a Good Girl for him. He rubbed his cock in the cleft of my arse, back and forth faster until I was begging him to fuck me there, and then I felt him shudder and hot wet heat cover my back and drip down my arse.

His fingers swirled through the mess he'd made on me. "Little mess," he said, sounding extremely pleased with himself. "Go clean yourself up."

I gathered my ruined dress and my bra from the floor. My legs were shaking and I was still breathing hard, trembling from the orgasms he'd given me.

He was tucked back in and zipped, lounging against his desk and inspecting me with a satisfied gleam in his eyes.

Some boldness, the same boldness that had led me on Monday to strip in front of him, had me tell him, "Sir, you have a meeting in about five minutes." I wanted to see if he could be rattled. The entire office stank of sex and there was cum and spilled coffee on the carpet.

The corner of his mouth lifted. "I know. Use my bathroom over there," he said and pointed to the discreet panel that opened a door to his private bathroom.

I tried to walk there with dignity, but I was just glad I didn't fall down, I was so exhausted from the intensity of the fucking he'd given me. My cunt felt bruised and blissful, aching already to have him back again.

Inside the bathroom, I studied myself in the mirror. The slap on my face had already faded to a faint blush. I had finger size bruises on my hips that I stroked reverently.

He had a shower stall, and I used the hand shower and blissful hot water to quickly clean myself up. The water almost stung on my cunt, but then ebbed to a pleasurable warmth. I thought of being fucked in here. It was a big stall, designed for his height, and I imagined him pinning me up against the wall, fucking me under the rain shower effortlessly.

Then I had the problem of being clean and naked with nothing to wear. I looked around frantically. There was a cupboard which held expensive toiletries, another with towels and then a small drawer which had a bathrobe neatly folded inside.

I pulled it on and tried my best to detangle my hair where he'd pulled it into an absolute disaster. There was nothing I could do about my lips, half my make-up gone in a sweaty dishevelled mess.

He was right. I was a little mess.

Just as I was about to open the door and go out, I heard knocking and then voices. The 4pm meeting. I shrank back, unsure what to do.

Was I supposed to stay hidden in his bathroom? There was no way I could go out and be caught by the senior managers who had been called in. He had told me to use the bathroom to clean up, and I didn't know if I would displease him by staying inside.

Then there was a knock on the bathroom door and it slid open; I'd forgotten to lock it! Mr Perrington looked in through a narrow crack. "Hmm," he said, examining me in my borrowed bathrobe. "Take this."

He tossed something at me and I caught it before it could crack on the bathroom floor. It was an iPad.

"If you're good, little mess," he said, his voice dropping to a murmur so that only I could hear him, "after this is over, I'll fuck you."

"I can't go out in —" I began but he just stared at me until I stopped protesting and nodded my head meekly.

"Hmm," he said again, and this time his voice had that same throaty rumble that promised sex. Promised and delivered. "Wait."

So I waited. I flipped through some websites, played some pointless games. Mostly, I stood in front of the mirror, trying to see if my arse was really pink where he'd spanked me, or running my hands over those marvellous big-spanned marks he'd left on my hips.

He didn't bother knocking the next time, just slid the door open. I'd stopped wearing the bathrobe in the warmth of the bathroom, so I stood there completely naked. Even the silk stockings which were, I was pleased to discover, not torn despite the vigorous fucking, were rolled up carefully by the sink.

"Good," he said when he saw me standing there naked except for the red heels I'd chosen for work that day. "Come out here and sit on my cock."

I followed him obediently out to his office. I hadn't really noticed before that his office had floor to ceiling windows. Not noticed them the way I did now that I was utterly naked and walking past them. I wondered if anyone else outside could see us. If anyone was watching.

I didn't care.

Not when Mr Perrington kicked out his big office chair and sprawled into it, all confidence and strength. He unzipped his pants again and drew out his cock. My mouth watered. I almost fell to my knees there, except he patted the armrests instead.

"Climb up," he said. "Keep your shoes on."

It was harder than I'd imagined and I was so grateful my roommate had bugged me into doing yoga with her. I needed the flexibility for what he wanted, for me to kneel astride his chair, my hands on his shoulders — they were so broad and steady under my touch — and to hold myself just above him.

I couldn't see how we would fuck. But then he reached behind and smacked my arse again, and I realised we weren't fucking yet. My cunt throbbed with desire and I wanted to sink down on to his waiting cock, but he wouldn't let me. Instead he drew me down against his chest and smacked my arse again and again until it was stinging and sore and so hot, I thought my skin was on fire.

"Have you earned a fucking," he asked as if he was asking me to make him a cup of coffee.

I nodded eagerly. I'd forgotten everything that I'd promised myself at the beginning of the week. To be a good girl who did the right thing and made sensible decisions. He scrambled my brain, made me seethe with desire for sex. I wanted him. Wanted him to control me, to dominate me, to own me.

I wanted to be fucked so badly. I wanted to please him.

"Sir," I said, "Please, I know I was bad, please," and he drove his hand again on the firm curve of my arse. It was fire, exquisite intense fire. Then his hands were on my breasts, lifting one to his mouth. He swirled his tongue over my nipple and I cried out with pleasure. His other hand worked into my wet cunt, three fingers diving in and out. It wasn't as good as his cock, still rock-hard beneath me just out of reach, but he was gorgeously rough, pushing and invading so that when I worked back on to his hand, he curved and slid his thumb inside and I was almost stretched full.

"Good," he murmured. "Good girl." Then he knocked my legs off the armrests so that suddenly, violently, I was sitting astride his lap, thighs wide-open, completely impaled by his massive cock. I could feel him right up to the top filling me and I ground down against the delicious pounding heat. He grabbed my arse, squeezing the tender flesh as he worked me up and down in a punishing rhythm.

This time, he came inside me, wet and thick. I was too lost in my third orgasm, fluttering tight around him as he licked and sucked my tits, his massive hand holding them both like they were little breasts, pushing them together so he could suck both nipples together, his tongue flicking and working them to intense sensitivity.

His pants were ruined by the fucking we'd done, and I braced myself for another of his punishments. But he only stood and stripped them off and his shirt too and threw them onto the desk. Then he pressed the intercom and called his senior P.A..

"Meredith, bring me a new suit. And something for Sabina to wear in the office."

I froze, wondering if I could go back to the bathroom to hide, or maybe behind a potted plant. I was naked and sitting on my boss' lap, and he was in just his black boxer-briefs.

He looked even better than I'd imagine, a dark watch of hair on his chest running down to the bulge in his briefs. His thighs were like tree trunks, and his belly firm and muscled. I wanted to spend the rest of the day exploring every delicious inch of him.

There was a polite knock on his door and then his senior P.A. came in, carrying several coat hangers of drycleaning. She looked completely unfazed to find me naked and sprawled across her boss' lap, or that he was half-naked himself too.

"Your blue suit, a new shirt and a black dress in her size," she said, clipping the hangers to a discreet hook near the bathroom door. "Do you need a tie?"

Mr Perrington shook his head. "That will be all," he said and Meredith inclined her head and strode out.

I wondered just how many naked women had been in the same position as me. If Meredith had. I felt suddenly insanely jealous.

"Hush," soothed my boss, sensing my sudden tension. He nibbled the back of my neck and I sighed and nestled into his arms.

The dress Meredith had bought was a fabulous black wrap that hugged all my curves and clung to my thighs. It felt expensive and when I caught sight of the designer label tag, I gasped. "This is worth more than my monthly salary," I said.

"Hmm," murmured Mr Perrington, turning me around slowly and raking his gaze up and down my body in a way that left no doubt he liked the dress. "Keep it."

When I got home that evening, my roommate Trissy gaped at the dress. "Honey, which bitch at a shop did you have to kill to get that?" she asked.

For a split second I considered telling her everything. The job that had turned out to be something far darker and more erotic than any ordinary work flirtation. The way I had come apart clinging to the desk, terrified and turned on.

Mr Perrington hadn't forbidden me from telling anyone. Yet, I felt like I owed him my obedience even here at home. "A really great sale," I said at last. "It was the last sample size they had."

That night, lying in my cheap little apartment room, I touched myself furtively, brushing my hand over the bruises he'd left on me, working my fingers down to my clit. I was wet at the memories of the fucking he'd given me and so horny, but it felt different without him there.

Disobedient.

I shoved my hands under my pillow, rolled over on to my stomach and forced myself to go to sleep without the relief of an orgasm.

When I turned up on Friday, his office was empty. He'd had a full day of meetings scheduled but now they were all updated to postponed. I lingered at my desk, checking my emails and trying to figure out what had happened.

There was a knock at the door and I spun round, hopeful.

It was Meredith, carrying some paperwork and files. She was dressed as always tres chic, her red curls caught up in a tight bun and a dark green suit that made her look even more gorgeous. She swept in and put the files down on my small desk, and tapped the paperwork on top.

"Now that Mr Perrington has confirmed your probationary period, you'll need to sign a few more documents," she said smoothly.

"Documents?" I echoed weakly. I picked them up to flip through. There was a non-disclosure agreement, a health review, and at the back, a detailed checklist that made me blush bright, bright red.

Flogging. Handcuffs. Paddles. Nipple clamps. Exhibitionism.

Some of the terms I knew but some of them were complete mysteries. I realised that this was an entire world of pain and pleasure that I knew nothing about.

I picked up a pen with trembling fingers and signed blindly. At the checklist, I looked plaintively at Meredith. "What if I don't know what some of these things are?" I asked.

She jabbed a finger at a few of them and said, "just cross these out and you'll probably be fine." She paused. "He knows what he's doing, if that helps."

I took a deep breath and followed her advice. I wasn't sure what I wanted, only that the experience the day before had left me more satisfied than I'd ever been in my life.

"Why me?" I blurted as she gathered up the papers and headed to the door.

She turned back and looked me up and down. Compared to her, I felt severely underdressed in just a plain off-the-rack suit skirt and simple blouse. I definitely didn't have her stunning looks.

"If you're wondering," she said, "If I ever provided these additional services to Mr Perrington, the answer is no. I was the one who suggested hiring an in-house source rather than relying on contractors."

"Hookers?" I said, my cheeks burning.

Meredith raised one perfectly pencilled eyebrow. "Extremely well paid and talented escorts," she corrected. "Women who know their worth."

"How did you know that I would be…"

Meredith smirked. "I've always been good at spotting talent," she said and then she was gone, leaving me alone in an echoing office.

I didn't have much work to do. All the meetings had already been rescheduled by Meredith and I realised the little bits of work I had been given earlier that week were of minor importance. Fetching coffee, typing up memos, fucking the boss…

Would I have taken the job if Meredith had been upfront at the job interview? I sat down in my boss' empty office chair and pressed my face against the leather, breathing in deep to see if I could smell that rich musk scent of him.

I knew then that if I had met Mr Perrington at the interview, I would have said yes. I'd say yes over and over, and that frightened me. Shouldn't I be running scared from an office where — thinking how everyone's gazes had swept over me politely — I'd been hired as the boss' fucktoy?

I went home, melancholy. There was no message from him, nothing. Just a sudden business trip and I was left behind like furniture.

Saturday night, Trissy tried to get me to go out clubbing with her. "You have that new dress! Come on, you'll definitely hit something tasty."

But all I wanted was for Monday to come faster. The thought of picking up some random and discovering that sex had been ruined for me was just depressing. I wanted Mr Perrington, not some drunk guy pawing at my breasts and grunting over me. I wanted a man who knew how to make my whole body quiver and come apart on his fingers, who could pound into me until I thought I would come apart.

Then Sunday morning, while Trissy snored drunkenly in her room, I ate dry cereal and stared at the TV, sunk in misery. Despite all the paperwork I'd signed and what Meredith had said, I felt certain that I would return on

Monday and find my work pass cancelled and a final pay cheque.

The doorbell buzzed and I trudged over to open it. A huge bouquet of dark red roses was being carried carefully by a delivery man. "Is there a Sabina here?" he asked, holding the flowers out.

I took them and buried my face in the petals. Their fragrance was heavenly. Tucked in among the blooms was a small card. I opened it up and read *Be on time* scrawled in Mr Perrington's familiar ink.

The rest of Sunday, I spent in my room where the perfume of the roses was intoxicating, almost overwhelming. Trissy demanded to know who my anonymous admirer was and I told her I had no idea.

"Maybe it's someone from Quant," she guessed. "You could get lucky and pick up a rich boyfriend."

I shook my head. "The place is full of overworked stuffed shirts," I said. "I don't think anyone there's noticed me."

I didn't know quite why I wasn't willing to say anything. Just that whatever this strange new arrangement with Mr Perrington was, I wanted fewer people to know.

It felt exciting and private. Dangerous when I thought about that list I'd trustingly signed. What would I allow him to do to me?

On Monday, I would find out.

3

———

I woke up early so I could shave everything. Absolutely everything on my body but my hair which I'd left in a deep conditioner so that it feel sleek and soft across my shoulders. I'd dug around in my wardrobe for the sexiest bra I had, pairing it again with the hand-washed silk stockings that I'd carefully put out to dry. I didn't want anything else on my skin again but silk.

Pulling those on over my smooth legs and clipping the garter belt onto them, I wanted to keep running my hands up and up my body, let them delve between my thighs and touch myself. But I also wanted *him* to touch me there first.

Every part of me felt ready. I didn't know how I'd quite survive getting to the office by bus, when all I wanted to do was rub my legs together and moan at the wet slippery frisson between my freshly-shaved pussy.

I caught a cab, squirming in the back seat. I could afford it on my new salary, and I wanted to be fresh and uncrumpled when he saw me.

Meredith was in the lobby when I reached the office and she glanced me up and down and nodded slightly in approval. Now that I knew she'd chosen me from all the other women for her boss, her approval felt heavier and more important than before.

Bracing myself, I went to the office and knocked twice and waited.

"Enter," he called.

He was behind his desk, busy working on his laptop. When I came in, he barely looked at me but pointed over to my desk. I pouted a little, but obeyed.

There was a stack of documents to be collated and filed, all of them marked sensitive and eyes-only. I sat quietly working, shifting a little restlessly in my chair every now and then when I glanced up at my boss and he didn't look back.

Was he testing me? I chewed my bottom lip, worried. Did I have to provoke him in order to get myself ravished? I didn't want to piss him off, thinking of the controlled power in his hands when he'd spanked me. But I also wanted to see that same fire unleashed onto me.

Finally he pushed back his chair and strode over to where I was meekly sorting papers.

He leaned down, his hands balanced on my desk and spun my chair around so I was suddenly under his body.

My nipples tightened at his very presence. "You're early today," he said. "That pleases me."

"Thank you, Sir," I said in a throaty whisper. I wanted to reach up and draw him down onto me, to kiss that generous wide mouth but something in his gaze had me pinned, breathless, to my chair. The hunger in his eyes.

"Are you… satisfied with your new job requirements?" he asked.

I nodded and he smiled, showing his teeth. They were sharp and very white. I wanted to feel them bite down my breasts, feel the sharp edges teasing my nipples.

My obedience must have pleased him for he lifted me up almost entirely. Just swooped his hands under my arse and lifted me against him, my skirt riding up so that suddenly I had my legs wrapped around his waist and he was carrying me back to his desk.

He pushed aside the computer and papers on the desk leaving it partly cleared. It was an enormous desk and I could lie completely back on it. I didn't want to unwrap my legs from around him, didn't want to let go of the sensation of being overwhelmed by him. It was heady.

But then he pushed my skirt higher up my thighs, over my hips and spread my knees. His face was between my thighs, his mouth tasting me before I could even gasp. I felt him smile against my shaved cunt, then the long wet warm lick of his tongue down the sensitive folds.

He was toying with me, tormenting me with every slide that came around but not quite to my clit. He tugged gently on the hood, licked delicately and then roughly and never directly on it until I was a writhing, moaning mess under him, begging him to let me come.

"Not yet," he said and undid his pants. I felt him slide home again with the same pain-pleasure burn of the stretch but this time, I was eager, avid to have him inside me. I wanted that massive cock even if it tore me apart. I lifted my back and worked myself down onto his cock, biting my lip to stop from screaming at how good it felt.

Then he was fucking me again, the demanding pounding of his desire sending my body shaking with every slam of his body onto mine.

I wanted to be pressed to him, but he was ruthless, pushing me back down onto the desk and spreading my legs even wider so he could pound in harder and deeper. He held my hands down and I struggled helplessly against his strength. That seemed to drive him even wilder, his thrusts growing erratic — and I liked it. I loved it. I struggled and bucked under him, moaning and whimpering and then for just one glorious moment, his hands were at my throat, closing.

He was pushing me back down into the desk, pushing my chin back so hard I saw stars. I couldn't breathe, couldn't do anything except choke on the slow squeezing at my throat, the burn of breath denied.

And every pounding, every stroke coming harder and faster into my cunt felt heated and darker, as if he would fuck me until I passed out. Fuck me after I passed out. And I wanted it.

I thrashed under him, feeling my body let go and then he was coming, filling me up and letting go at the same time so I could suck in shaky staggering breaths.

He was no softer, still hard inside me. I moved cautiously, my throat burning and my cunt aching but still desperate to feel him. I had come but it had been an intense cold burning orgasm and I wanted the gentleness I sensed inside him now.

He ran his hand over my throat. "You're bruised," he said and kissed the bruises tenderly. I turned my neck so he could kiss the other side. He moved gently inside me, and then one hand went to my clit and played sweetly there, little strokes that worked in rhythm with the kisses he was lavishing on my neck, my chest, my breasts.

My second orgasm of the morning was light and sugar-sweet, a flutter that made him shiver when I came again around his cock.

Then he pulled out and I made a little whimper of disappointment. He smiled and pressed a kiss to my mouth. "Good girl," he said.

I pulled my skirt down and tried to re-arrange myself to look presentable. It was nearly lunch and I couldn't see how I would make it to the nearest sandwich shop with his seed still sticky on my thighs.

"Sir?" I asked, trying to look away from his intense gaze so I could speak.

"You can ask one question now," he said. "Then I want you to go to the bathroom and shower. Clean yourself completely."

I melted inside thinking what he might want me to be clean for. Completely clean.

One question, my lust-scrambled mind reminded me.

"Sir, what do you expect from me?" I asked.

"I expect obedience," he said. He tipped my face up by my chin, his strong fingers holding me stock-still. He seemed to look right within me, as if he was messing parts of me that no-one else had seen, not even myself.

And he liked what he saw. That was what frightened me the most, standing there still light-headed from the sex we'd had. He wanted me, this huge rich obscenely good in bed man. He wanted to fuck me and have me and when I said *yes*, he liked that even more.

And I wanted to say yes.

I opened my mouth to ask another question but he held up one warning finger. "One question, I said. Go and shower."

In the bathroom, bathing and cleaning myself everywhere I could reach, I thought again what he meant by obedience.

Was it too much? Looking at my wet gleaming body in the mirror, the marks of his hands leaving a startling necklace of bruises around my throat, I was afraid.

I should leave, I thought. It would be safer.

Then he silently opened the door. His shirt was unbuttoned, tie off. His sleeves were rolled up, showing off his thickly muscled forearms. He was coiling something in his hands.

A whip, I realised with a start.

Then I felt myself growing wet with desire, my whole body trembling at the way he flicked it casually across his hands, toying with the long plaited leather of it.

Leave or stay?

"Yes, Sir," I said obediently.

AFTERWORD

Thank you for reading ***Spanking the Good Girl***! I hope you enjoyed this steamy office punishment story. If you'd like to read what happened the next week with Sabina and Sir, please leave a review on Amazon. Reader reviews make all the difference, so once again, thank you.

The Killer's Mate

Catherine has lost her sweet boyfriend to a brutal werewolf attack. Newly turned, she swears revenge on Duncan of clan Longbow for all the pain he has brought her.

When he claims that she is his destined mate, her animal side responds savagely to his call, her body overwhelmed by lust.

Can she resist his command or will she give in to her longing of her destiny? A dark erotic romance of enemies-to-lovers, The Killer's Mate will leave you trembling with desire.

ABOUT THE AUTHOR

Clara Colt lives with her family, cats and one very confused dog near the beach.

She loves to hear from readers at clara@claracolt.com